Card Tricks

JON MESSENGER

Copyright © 2012 Jon Messenger

All rights reserved.

ISBN: 1480076724
ISBN-13: 978-1480076723

ACKNOWLEDGMENTS

To my editor, Cynthia Shepp, without whom I'd still be using far too many commas in my writing. For more information on her writing, follow her at cynthiashepp.wordpress.com

Most importantly, to my loving family. My beautiful wife of six years, Jacquelyn, and our handsome son, Alistair. Without your support, I would have never followed my dreams of writing.

Other Works by Jon Messenger:

Novels:
Rage

Brink of Distinction Series:
Burden of Sisyphus
Fall of Icarus
Purge of Prometheus

Short Stories:
Canyon Bound
Card Tricks

Follow the writings of Jon Messenger and discover exclusive content:
Twitter: @JonMessenger
Facebook: www.facebook.com/JonMessengerAuthor

CHAPTER ONE

A lady stepped into line at the ATM directly behind Joey Scaglione. Shifting his over-the-shoulder bag, Joey stepped out of the way, letting the woman pass go before him.

"Thank you," she beamed, as she stepped forward.

Joey nodded wordlessly and resumed his place at the back of the line.

As the patron at the front of the line walked away, the woman stepped forward and slid her card into the slot. Concealing the keypad with her body, she inputted her access code. She didn't need to bother concealing her password. Joey wasn't paying any attention to what she was doing. Instead, he was glancing up and down the street, watching the disinterested pedestrians pass them by.

The ATM wasn't cleverly concealed on the street, sandwiched as it was in a brick wall between an all-night convenience store and a liquor store. The sidewalk in front of it was never empty but people repeatedly walked by the machine without so much as a second glance. Aside from tourists, like the woman in front of Joey wearing the 'I Love Belltown' t-shirt, the ATM was hardly used at all. It was for this reason that Joey preferred it.

Whirring to life, the ATM dispensed the woman's money. She gave a cursory glance over her shoulder at Joey, who ran a hand through his slicked-back hair and flashed a disarming smile. Smiling sheepishly, the woman retrieved her money and stepped away from the machine.

Letting the smile fade from his face, Joey looked around once more. No one spared him a glance as they passed, hurrying as they were to get home after a long day's work. Most were ending their day as the sun set over Belltown. For the few, like Joey, their days were just beginning.

Turning back to the ATM, Joey pulled aside his leather jacket and retrieved the wallet from his back pocket.

The blue screen illuminated his face as it advised him to insert his credit or debit card.

Reaching into one of the side pockets of his wallet, he pushed aside his debit card and instead pulled out a thin orange card, one slightly smaller than a traditional business card. Instead of inserting it into the awaiting slot, Joey held it in front of the screen.

For long seconds, nothing happened. Joey frowned and held the card closer to the machine.

"Come on," he said, glancing over his shoulder again.

Just when he was reaching the end of his patience, the card started heating up in his hands. The corners of the card curled and browned, and wisps of smoke rose from its edges.

On the ATM screen, the words flickered and the image rolled. For a moment, the request to insert a credit card remained. Suddenly, they disappeared and were replaced by another familiar screen.

"Please remove your cash," it read.

The machine whirred and the cash dispenser opened. A stack of twenty-dollar bills emerged.

Joey released the card in his hand with a hiss as it burned down to his fingers like a used match. The orange card fluttered down to the ground, landing amidst the other debris against the brick wall.

Reaching out, Joey removed the money from the ATM. Flipping through them, he counted the stack of ten bills before slipping them into his wallet.

Glancing over his shoulder, he checked to make sure he hadn't been observed. Joey adjusted the satchel over his shoulder and replaced his wallet before shoving his hands in his pockets and merging with the crowd walking past.

Coming to rest on the ground against the wall, the orange card rolled in the evening breeze, flipping face upward. Through the singed discoloration, the dark black letters stared up at the fading sunlight.

"Advance To Go. Collect $200."

CHAPTER TWO

As Joey arrived at the card shop he found the owner standing impatiently by the front door, staring at his watch. Joey tapped the glass, startling the man.

"You're late," the man said gruffly, his voice muted by the glass door. "I almost closed up for the night."

Joey pulled the door open, hearing the jingling of the bell above him. "I'm glad you didn't. It would have put a damper on my evening plans."

The owner walked behind the glass display counter. Stacked within the case were a number of cards, each entombed in individual hard plastic cases. Joey walked down the counter, his eyes never leaving the stacks as he scanned the merchandise. The owner organized the cards neatly by type, ranging from 'Yu-Gi-Oh' in the front, through 'Pokemon' in the middle, and ending with the more collectible 'Magic the Gathering' cards near the end.

Joey frowned, as nothing special caught his eye. "You have my usual?"

The owner reached behind the front case and pulled out a small brown paper bag. "They get delivered like clockwork. You going to buy anything else today?"

Glancing back at the display, Joey's eyes fell on one of the 'Yu-Gi-Oh' cards. A hefty price tag was scribbled on a sticker affixed to the plastic case. Ignoring the price, Joey looked down and locked eyes with the 'Blue-Eyes White Dragon', its long curved neck and bullet head turned to the side. As his hand touched the glass of the display case, Joey felt a surge of power as he connected with the cards within. He quickly drew his hand away as though electrocuted.

"No," Joey stammered. "Just the usual."

The owner shrugged and tipped over the bag. Shrink-wrapped stacks of orange and yellow Monopoly cards tumbled onto the counter. Nodding, Joey counted the stacks.

"How much?" Joey asked.

"Thirty," the owner replied, "same as every week."

Joey smiled and pulled out a pair of twenty-dollar bills from his wallet. Sliding them across the table, the owner frowned.

"You never have exact change, you know that? No matter how many tens I give you back, you always come in here with nothing but twenties."

Joey shrugged. "When the ATM starts giving tens, I'll start bringing you exact change."

Setting his satchel on the countertop, Joey lifted the front flap. Within, dozens of special pockets were stitched into the inner lining, each large enough to hold a small stack of playing or tabletop cards. He stuffed the Monopoly cards into a series of larger pockets while the owner pulled out the ten-dollar bill.

"What do you do with all those Monopoly cards?" the owner asked.

"You ask me that every time I come in here," Joey responded with a smile. He closed the satchel and slung it across his chest.

"And you never give me a straight answer."

Joey laughed. "Then why ruin a good thing now?"

The owner sighed and followed Joey as they walked

to the front of the store. Joey stepped through ahead of the man, hearing the tinkling of the bell above him as the door opened. The owner propped the door open with his body and absently turned the sign on the door from 'open' to 'closed'.

"Same time next week?" the owner asked.

Joey turned as he walked away, so that he was walking backward down the street. "Same time every week."

With a wave, the owner closed and locked the door behind him.

CHAPTER THREE

There was a long line outside the bar as Joey approached. A large bouncer pressed into a three-piece suit stood at the entrance, blocking the eager crowd with his girth and a velvet rope. The posh men and women waiting impatiently in line were dressed far too nicely for this part of town. Cocktail dresses and business casual attire were the outfits of the day. The ladies were adorned with sparkling necklaces and earrings. Even the men wore ridiculously expensive watches.

Joey seemed out of place, wearing only a loose fitting pair of jeans and his leather jacket. The only accessories were a pair of thick leather bracelets concealed under his jacket. Reaching nearly from his wrists to his elbows, the bracers gave Joey the appearance of renaissance chic. Few people knew that they served a much more important purpose than merely fashion accessories.

Walking past the bouncer, Joey approached a musty concrete stairwell that led down to the building's basement. The smell in the narrow stairwell was atrocious; a nauseating mixture of urine and vomit. Stepping over unidentifiable pools on the stairs, Joey walked to their gloomy bottom and knocked on the heavy wooden door.

"Who is it?" a rough voice asked from the other side.

"It's Joey," he replied, glancing back up the stairs. "Let me in."

Joey heard a heavy lock being pulled aside and the door creaked open. The man behind the door looked frail compared to the muscular bouncer at the building's main entrance, but Joey felt more afraid of this man than he did his larger counterpart.

"They're in the back," the man at the door announced. He slammed the door shut behind Joey and slid the deadbolt back into place.

The room was dark, with only a softly glowing exposed light bulb hanging in the center of the room. The majority of illumination in the room spilled from a doorway at the back of the storage room. From the harsh light, Joey was able to weave through the stacked crates. Heavy dance music escaped from a stairwell to his right, which led up to the club itself.

Joey approached the back room cautiously, listening to the gruff laughter and conversation that escaped. Stepping into the doorway, he forced a smile at the trio sitting around the table.

"Welcome back," the man across the table said. The man's square jaw flexed as he ground his teeth together in a poor imitation of a smile. "We didn't think you were going to make it today."

"And miss a chance to take your money?" Joey replied confidently. "I wouldn't miss that for the world."

Slinging his satchel over his head, he hung the bag from the top of his chair and took his seat. Pulling out his wallet, he withdrew five of the twenty-dollar bills and laid them on the table.

The man to his left – Joey never could remember any of their names – took his cash and counted out a stack of black, red, blue, and white chips. Sliding them in front of Joey, the man stashed Joey's money in a bank cashier's bag sitting on the corner of the table.

Cashing in only a hundred dollars, Joey's stack was far smaller than the others at the table but he wasn't overly concerned. It wasn't the starting money that he cared about; it was how much he would take by the end of the night.

"The game is five card draw," the man across from him announced, as he shuffled a crisp new deck of cards. "We play this every week, so you all know the rules."

The man deftly passed around the cards face down. Waiting until they had all been dispensed, Joey picked up his stack and examined his hand. Frowning, he knew this hand wasn't going to be a winner for him. He quickly folded his hand as the betting began.

The next hand, the dealing was passed around the table and the man to Joey's right now passed out the cards. Joey again quickly discarded his hand, losing only his miniscule ante.

Despite his conservative playing style, the others barely took note of Joey's bets. They drank beer and joked with one another freely, as though they were all fast friends. In truth, Joey wasn't sure how well the others knew one another, only that he only saw them once a week for their high-stakes poker night.

As the cards were handed to Joey for dealing, he smiled confidently. His fingers flew over the cards as he shuffled the deck. Nimbly separating the deck again, he held the cards in five equal stacks before reshuffling the cards in a new order. The others watched him impatiently. The first night, they had been adequately impressed by his skills with a deck of cards. Now, they all frowned at the delay of their game.

"Get on with it," the man to Joey's left demanded. "Cut the crap."

Joey shuffled the cards one last time before dealing five cards to each of them. His fingers were a blur as he slung the cards in front of each of the other players. Blinded by his speed, they never noticed the cards that he dropped for himself from the bottom of the deck.

Picking up their hands, they stared at their cards. Joey suppressed a smile as he looked down at the straight in his hand. Around the table, the other men betted their hands and Joey quickly matched their bets. When they were done, none of the men had folded, just as Joey had hoped.

"How many, gentlemen?" Joey asked.

They dropped cards on the table, which Joey quickly replaced with cards from the deck. Taking no cards himself, betting resumed around the table.

When it made it back to Joey, he shrugged. "I'm all in," he declared, as he pushed his entire stack of chips into the center of the table.

The man to his left threw down his cards in disgust and Joey could see the crestfallen look mirrored on the face of the man to his right. Only the man across from Joey smirked at the bet.

"I call," the man across from him said, pushing out nearly a quarter of his own chips.

"Too rich for me," the man to Joey's right exclaimed, dropping his cards face down on the table.

"Show me what you got," the man said.

Joey smiled. "I dealt, you show."

The man laid down his cards face up and spread them apart so everyone could see.

"Three eights."

Joey pursed his lips and nodded slowly. The man, misreading his reaction, reached out to the pile of chips on the table. Shaking his head softly, Joey dropped his own cards onto the table.

"Straight," he explained. "I believe those chips are mine."

The man across from him scowled but withdrew his hands. Joey raked the chips into a pile in front of him and began stacking them in like quantities. The night had just started, and Joey's one hundred dollars was already doubled.

The game continued over the next few hours. The pile in front of Joey grew steadily larger. He won small hands that would draw less attention to his winnings, while losing some key larger hands. The numbers constantly flew through his mind as he calculated his losses against his gains. The chips grew from two hundred to nearly four hundred as two o'clock approached.

The cards were dealt to Joey from the man across the table. Slipping them into his hands, he examined his cards. He heart pounded when he looked at the cards in his hand. A pair of kings and an ace stared back at him, coupled with a set of insignificant lower numbered cards.

When betting came around to him, Joey bet a safe amount, not too much to drive away the partially drunk gamblers. The others took his bait and threw nearly another hundred dollars into the pot.

"How many cards?" the dealer asked.

Joey dropped his two lower cards onto the table. "Give me two."

The dealer watched Joey sternly as he dealt him the two cards. Joey picked them up and slid them into his hand, but barely acknowledged the numbers.

As soon as the man across the table looked down to his own cards, Joey slipped the two new cards under his leather bracer. From their concealed location, he drew a king and ace of hearts out and placed them in his hand. Instead of the pair of kings he previously held, Joey now looked down on a full house, with kings and aces.

"I'm all in," Joey announced when it got to his turn. He pushed his significant stack, over four hundred dollars, into the center of the table.

The man to his left frowned and eyed Joey warily. Not able to sense any bluffing, the man dropped his cards face down on the table.

"Don't let him get away with this crap," he said to the other two.

The man across from Joey stared at him intently, his eyes boring through Joey's stony façade.

"I call," the man said, pushing forward a significant portion of his own chip stack.

"I call too," the man to Joey's right answered immediately afterward.

Joey's eyes lit up at the thirteen hundred dollars piled high in the middle of the table. His hands grew sweaty, knowing this was his moment. Not only would this be his winning hand for the night, it would be the last night he spent with these particular gamblers. After a large victory like the one he was about to have, he wasn't eager to show his face around these disgruntled gentlemen again any time soon.

"Show them," the stern-faced man across from Joey demanded.

The man to his right laid down his cards first. "Three of a kind," he proclaimed.

The dealer scoffed at the exposed cards and turned his attention to Joey. In the back of his mind, Joey could sense the palpable danger hovering in the air over the table.

"Your turn," he told Joey.

Joey swallowed hard and laid down his cards. Three kings and a pair of aces stared up from the table. The man to Joey's right exhaled sadly, knowing he lost his money.

"Kings over aces," Joey explained.

The man across from him frowned deeply and furrowed his brow. Joey mistook the look as one of angry defeat and started reaching for the chips.

"It's interesting that you have kings over aces," the man explained. His tone froze Joey's hands in midstride. "Especially with the king of hearts. See, I've got a flush. Hearts, too."

The man laid down his cards on the table, revealing five hearts staring up. At the end of the row of cards, the highest card in his set was the king of hearts.

"Seems there are suddenly two kings of hearts in the deck," the man said dangerously.

Joey laughed nervously. "What are the chances?"

The man scooted back his chair and cracked his knuckles. "He cheated. Grab him."

Before Joey could respond, the man to his left

tackled him like a defensive linebacker. Joey let loose a high-pitched scream as the man knocked him clear of his chair.

CHAPTER FOUR

They held Joey's arms behind his back while the man who had sat across from him removed his jacket. Joey could feel their fingers digging into the skin around his wrists, pulling free the concealed cards from his bracers.

"Seems you were right, Bob," one of the men said, as he held up the pair of cards Joey had slipped into his bracers during the game. "He's been cheating."

Bob stepped in front of Joey. He could smell the man's moist heavy breath carrying across the space between them.

"I knew you were doing too good to be playing fair," Bob remarked.

"Guys," Joey laughed softly, "this is all just a big misunderstanding. I can explain…"

Bob lashed out, punching Joey just beneath his left eye. His head snapped backward from the impact, smashing into the face of one of the men behind him. Aching now both in his face and the back of his head, Joey stomped on the ground and cringed.

"The eye?" Joey exclaimed. "Right in the eye? Are you serious?"

Bob drove his fist into Joey's gut, knocking the wind from his lungs. Joey collapsed onto the ground and the men behind him released their grip. Coughing painfully, he laid his head down on the cool, wooden floor.

"Better," he croaked.

Rubbing his knuckles, Bob knelt down so he could

look into the one eye of Joey's that looked up toward the ceiling.

"You've been coming here for weeks, never winning big but always walking out of here ahead. I have to figure you've been cheating since day one, which means that every penny you walked out of here with is our money. I want my money back!"

Joey pushed himself off the ground with one arm, while clutching his bruised stomach with the other. He coughed again, letting a thin line of spittle fall to the floor.

"I don't have a lot with me, except for what is sitting on the table. You can take all of that. It's yours."

Bob nodded. "Oh, that's already mine. As soon as I knew you were cheating, you stopped owning any of the money on the table. I'm not talking about getting that money back. I'm talking about the rest of it. I figure you walked away with about three hundred dollars each week. That adds up to around twelve hundred dollars you owe us."

Joey wiped his mouth with the back of his hand and rocked back onto his knees. "I don't have twelve hundred dollars."

"Go through his man-purse," Bob ordered, pointing to Joey's over-the-shoulder bag hanging from his chair.

"It's a satchel..." Joey started to correct, before getting punched in the stomach again.

Doubling over, he rolled onto the ground and watched as they opened his bag. Bob and one of the other men pulled out handfuls of the gaming cards stashed in their pockets.

"What is this?" Bob asked, dumbfounded.

"He doesn't have any money in here," the other man said.

"I can see that," Bob roared. Turning to Joey, he held up some of the cards. "What are these? Are you one of those losers who make believe with dragons and elves? Is this the type of person we've let play at our table?"

"Please put those back," Joey groaned from the ground.

Bob looked at the cards with a renewed interest. "Why? Are they worth something?"

Joey shook his head. "Not to you, they're not."

Tossing the cards onto the table, Bob looked at the other man still standing behind Joey. "Check his wallet. See how much he can pay us now."

Joey didn't fight it as the man lifted his jacket and pulled the wallet from his back pocket. His mind whirled as the thug opened his wallet and withdrew the seventy dollars within.

"It's not much, but it's a start," the man told Bob, as he held up the cash.

"He's right," Bob said, kneeling down in front of Joey again. "It's not much."

"There's more," Joey blurted.

"Let me guess. At your house? All I have to do is let you go and you'll bring us the full twelve hundred?"

Joey shook his head and rolled into a seated position. "No, there's more in my wallet."

Bob looked to the man holding his wallet. The man shook his head.

"There's nothing else in there," Bob scowled. "Don't lie to me."

"There's a hidden compartment in the wallet with another stack of bills," Joey explained. "Let me see the wallet and I'll get it for you."

He could see the hesitation in Bob's eyes as he stole a glance at the men standing around him.

"What harm can I do with a wallet?" Joey exclaimed. "There's still three of you and only one of me."

"Give it to him," Bob conceded.

Joey took the wallet and pulled out a set of business cards. Dropping them one after another onto the ground, he grinned as he found the card he was looking for.

Clutching it between his fingers, Joey held it up so Bob could read the front of the card. The back of the card was scrawled with flowing writing. From his perspective, Joey could read 'Vampire: the Eternal Struggle'.

"What is this?" Bob asked angrily, pointing at the gaming card in Joey's hand. "Another one of your loser cards?"

"It's not the card itself," Joey explained. "It's what's written on the card."

Bob squinted as he tried to read the title. Reading the single word across the top, Bob arched an eyebrow in confusion.

"Arson?"

Joey smiled. The card in his fingers heated supernaturally and the air above it danced in the heat.

"Yup," Joey responded. "Arson."

Sweeping the card downward, the wooden floor at his feet ignited in a wall of flames. Bob collapsed backward, shielding his eyes. The man with Joey's satchel staggered backward and tripped over one of the chairs.

Standing, Joey drove an elbow into the face of the man behind him. Screaming in anguish, the man fell to the floor. Taking a deep breath, Joey jumped through the flames, landing beside the poker table.

Untangling himself from the legs of the chair, the man with his satchel tried to stand but Joey's booted foot caught him under the chin. Reaching down, Joey retrieved his satchel and slid the few cards they had pulled out of the bag back into the satchel's main compartment. Grabbing the bank deposit bag from the table, Joey paused just long enough to collect his king and ace of hearts and replace them in his leather bracer.

A hand closed over Joey's ankle as he turned to leave. Bob rubbed his eyes with his free hand, trying to wipe away the afterglow that danced in front of his vision.

Joey stomped down with his free foot on Bob's wrist, immediately breaking his hold on Joey's ankle. Bob screamed and clutched his wrist as Joey jumped back through the flames and ran out the door.

"Get that son of a bitch!" he heard Bob yell after him, though none of the three in the room were in any condition to give chase.

Smirking as he passed from the illuminated back room into the dark storage room, Joey nearly ran into the wiry doorman. The man scowled and dropped a hand to his lower back, where he had a pistol concealed. Without thinking, Joey slammed his head into the bridge of the man's nose. The doorman fell to the floor, moaning in pain. Joey's hand jerked to his face and he furiously rubbed the growing knot on his forehead.

With the doorman lying between him and the door, Joey instead turned toward the stairwell that led to the club. Vaulting up the stairs, taking two or three at a time, he was nearly at the door at the top when the first gunshot rang out. Sparks flew from the concrete wall behind him and Joey threw his hands up around his face reflexively.

Turning the handle, Joey threw his shoulder into the door and nearly fell through into the club's back kitchen. Stumbling, trying to catch his footing, Joey hurried to the bump-through door and entered into the club.

The door swung outward behind one of the bars. A surprised bartender looked up but made no move to stop Joey. Stepping onto the bar, Joey ran its length toward the front of the club before jumping down, knocking down a pair of club patrons as he landed.

Despite the throbbing bass that passed from the speakers and through his temples, Joey could hear the yelling from behind him. Stealing a glance, he saw both Bob and the doorman staggering through the door behind the bar. They pointed at Joey as they spotted him pushing through the crowd.

Panicked, Joey raised his hands to his mouth and screamed at the top of his lungs.

"Fire!"

He expected a mob response to his cries but few heard him over the deafening music. Scowling, he pushed his way further toward the door. From the corner of his eye, he saw another option and changed directions.

Coming to a stop before the fire alarm, Joey turned

and made eye contact with Bob, just as the big man crested the top of the bar. Using his elbow to shatter the protective glass, Joey grabbed the fire alarm handle and pulled it downward.

A screeching cut through the music and blindingly bright strobe lights flashed overhead. Joey was most of the way to the front door before the wave of panic rolled through the crowd. The throng immediately drove toward the exit, crushing bodies against one another in an attempt to escape.

Joey rode the wave of fleeing patrons through the front door of the club. Rushing outside, using the frightened patrons for cover, Joey's exit went unnoticed by the large bouncer who was busy trying to stem the tide of fleeing people.

Free of the club, Joey turned down the road and disappeared into the night.

CHAPTER FIVE

The train ride back to the suburbs was slow. A faint throb remained in his eye and the skin around it had turned an ugly purple. He could have healed the injury but he chose not to. It was a good reminder of his carelessness tonight.

Staring out the window, he watched the sky turn from a deep black to a dark blue. Streaks of reds and yellows traced their way across the horizon as the sun began to crest the distant mountains.

Joey lowered his head back down and slipped his hand inside his satchel. The bank deposit bag was still unzipped, allowing him to wrap his fingers around the mound of bills concealed inside. He wanted nothing more than to pull the money free and count it but he knew the train wasn't the right place for counting nearly fifteen hundred dollars.

A commotion drew Joey's attention upward. The other people on the train, many who had the glassy expressions of those riding the train home after overly stimulating evenings, rushed to the far side of the passenger car. Leaning forward, Joey glanced past them and out the window.

In the distance, weaving its way between the tall skyscrapers, a streak of flame cut through the city. The front of the stream of fire was a brightly glowing ball, white hot and nearly blinding to watch. Within the cocoon of flames, a roughly human shape was silhouetted against the blazing inferno.

Joey frowned at the sight and sat back in his seat. Inferno, a trail of flames following him wherever he flew, swooped between another pair of buildings and disappeared from sight. The rest of the train passengers let loose a collective, disappointed sigh and returned to their seats. As the trailing flames died away behind Inferno, the city skyline was once again left bathed only in the light of the rising sun.

Getting off on the next stop, Joey walked away from the train station. The short walk to his subdivision took longer than it should have since Joey was hardly in a hurry.

The sun was rising over the taller buildings of Belltown by the time Joey arrived back at his townhouse. As he opened the front door, he heard the shower running upstairs.

"Hello?" a female voice called from the upstairs banister.

Joey walked forward until he could see the loft. His dark haired girlfriend leaned over the railing, her hair dripping wet and her body covered only by a towel wrapped around her midsection.

"It's just me, baby," Joey said with a smile.

Danica smiled down at her boyfriend. "I was worried you weren't going to make it home before I...oh my God, what happened to your eye?"

Joey shook his head, embarrassed. "It's nothing. The game just got a little rougher than I expected."

Danica frowned. "Did the game go well, at least?"

"I got a black eye, so the game didn't go great," Joey laughed. He pulled the bank deposit bag from his satchel. "I did come out on top, though."

"How much?" Danica asked excitedly.

"Just over fourteen hundred. I haven't had a chance to count it all yet."

Danica pushed back from the railing and walked toward the door at the end of the loft. "I need to finish getting ready for work. Grab some breakfast and I'll be down in a second."

Joey slung his satchel into one of the living room chairs and collapsed onto the couch. He didn't feel very hungry but he knew it would be a while until sleep came. He turned on the television, laid his head back on the couch cushions, and stared up at the ceiling

Soft footsteps creaked on the stairs and Joey raised his head. Danica was dressed in a silk blouse that was tucked into a form-fitting gray skirt. High-heeled knee-high boots accentuated her already tall and lithe frame. She sat down beside him and invited him to lean back into her. Nuzzling into the crook of her neck, she draped her arms over his shoulders and laid her head on his.

"I wish you didn't get beat up like that," she whispered.

"I know," Joey replied, feeling himself growing drowsy in her arms.

"You don't have to gamble," Danica offered. "We can get all the money we need out of the ATMs. You don't have to come home with black eyes."

"I know," Joey said again. "It's just...I don't do it for the money. I've been gambling since before the war. Since before I became a Super. It's a comfortable throwback to remind me I'm still normal."

Danica hugged him tightly. "You could do something more with your powers, instead of taking money out of ATMs or cheating at cards."

Joey frowned and unwound himself from Danica's arms. He sat upright on the couch and stared at her sternly.

"Please don't start that again," he said.

Danica pouted. "You have powers, Joey. You're a Super. You could be famous, just like the rest of them. You could have corporate sponsors giving you millions of dollars just for being you."

"I'm not like them," Joey replied. "I'm not a Super like Inferno or Wormhole or Strong Man. Hell, I'm not even as powerful as Supervillains like Razor or the Puppet Master. They have powers. I do parlor tricks with cards. I'm not even in the same league."

"But you could be! You were all friends in the war, when you were exposed. You got the same powers that they did!"

"Razor can cut through a steel vault door with the wave of his hand. Strong Man can punch through a building. A freaking building! What can I do?"

They sat in silence. Joey's frustration bled away, leaving him feeling sorry for his girlfriend. She meant well but she couldn't understand his inferiority complex when compared his powerful friends.

"I'm sorry," Joey said sadly. "I just can't get caught up in all that Superhero crap."

"But why not?" she begged. "Why can't you just be a hero?"

"Because having Superheroes has been terrible for Belltown. Every big city has a level of moral ambiguity; citizens that walk past crimes being committed because they feel like it's someone else's problem. In Belltown, they think that 'someone' should be a Superhero. They don't walk past crimes because they are indifferent. They walk past crimes and feel vindicated because they're sure any second now a Super is going to show up and save the day. They don't think that the majority of us can't move at super speeds. If Strong Man wants to show up at a crime, he has to get into a police car and fight through downtown traffic. The last thing this town needs is one more Super suddenly showing up. I can't perpetuate that bad cycle."

Danica leaned forward and kissed Joey on the cheek. "I love your moral high ground."

Joey smiled and kissed her on the lips. "You look great today, by the way."

"Thanks, sweetie. I'm going to be late to work if I don't leave now. Then I won't have any reason to dress up this nice."

He leaned forward and kissed her neck. "You can always dress up like a naughty librarian for me."

Danica laughed and slapped away his groping hands. "That's enough of that, Romeo. I have to go to work. Montrose International waits for no one, not even a hot secretary."

"Executive assistant," Joey corrected. "Alright. Go have fun at work."

She kissed him again before pushing herself off the couch. "Will you be home tonight, or are you going out?"

"I'll be here. I figured I could take you out somewhere nice for dinner." Joey touched the moneybag. "My treat."

"Damn right it is," Danica replied. She blew him a

kiss as she walked to the door. "I'll see you tonight. I love you."

"Love you, too," Joey replied, as he watched her leave.

Laying his head back on the couch again, he stared up at the ceiling and let the television drone on in the background.

CHAPTER SIX

As the phone rang, Joey looked up at the clock on the wall. The digital clock read 12:05. Rubbing his face, trying to remove the lines from the couch pillows, he reached to the end table and answered the phone.

"Hello?" he mumbled.

"Joey? Thank God you answered," Danica whispered. Her voice quivered as though on the edge of a breakdown.

"Danica? What's wrong?" Joey sat upright, suddenly very awake.

"There's something going on at the office." Joey could hear the tears in her voice. "The whole building is locked down. Paul went out earlier to see what was going on and he never came back. There's something moving in the hallway. It sounds so big!"

"Calm down, baby. Hold on, I'm turning on the news."

Joey picked up the remote and turned the channel. All the channels he flipped through had the same banner scrolling across the bottom.

"We bring you this breaking news as it happens," an announcer said, as Joey paused on a channel. "The Puppet Master has been spotted at the Montrose International building in Belltown. We go live now to Patricia Yakamoto, live on the scene. Hi, Patricia?"

The scene changed to a female reporter with the Montrose building framing the scene behind her. Around her, police established cordons and crouched behind their police cars.

"Thanks, Julie. I'm here at the Montrose International building in downtown Belltown. Here's what we know: at about eleven thirty today the Puppet Master entered the lobby of the Montrose building. Shortly thereafter, the first calls came in to the police. Police, SWAT, and even some National Guard representatives are on scene right now, but they've been unable to make contact with the Puppet Master."

"We understand that he has hostages. Is that correct?"

"What we've heard from the police spokesman is that a few people were able to escape the building when the Puppet Master first arrived but we haven't seen anyone else come out since. There are nearly a thousand people working among the forty-five floors."

The screen cut to a split screen, with Julie on one half and Patricia on the other. "Has he made any demands?"

"None so far, Julie. The police have been unable to get inside the building to speak with him because of one of his puppets blocking the doorway behind me."

The camera panned over Patricia's shoulder, showing the front of the building. Standing guard in front of the double doors was an animated front desk. The segmented sections of the desk jutted like legs and arms from its central core. Shredded drawers protruded along its length like spikes. On top of its frame, the receptionist's computer monitor rested with a humanoid face projected on its screen.

For a long moment Joey just stared at the television, the phone forgotten in his hand.

"Joey!" Danica hissed impatiently. Joey couldn't blame her for being panicked inside the building.

"I'm still here," he muttered.

"Is it bad?" she asked, the irritation replaced with nervousness.

"It's nothing you need to worry about. Just don't go outside. In fact, go lock the door to your office and don't open it for anyone. You hear me? Lock the door and stay in your office, no matter what."

"I hear someone coming," Danica cried. "Please come get me. Please, Joey! Oh God, someone's com…"

The phone line went dead in Joey's hand. "Hello?" he screamed into the receiver. "Hello?"

Joey hung up the phone and let it drop onto the floor.

"It's nothing to worry about," Joey rationalized. "One of the Supers will come along and take care of the Puppet Master. It's what they do. We just need to sit tight."

"We've noticed an absence of the Superheroes, Patricia," Julie announced on the television. "Where are Inferno, the Visionary, Brain, or Strong Man?"

Patricia nodded in the split screen. "We asked the police the same question but their answers have been vague. The information we're getting is that they have responded to an international crisis. When we asked the police spokesman about this we were informed that the police are formulating a plan to deal with the Puppet Master and his puppets."

Joey placed his hands on his hips and stared angrily at the screen.

"Figures," he growled.

CHAPTER SEVEN

Joey climbed to the top of the stairs, entered the bedroom, and walked to the closet. Pulling the doors open, he flipped on the light and stared at the top shelf. There, buried amongst the pillows and spare blankets, he could see the white cardboard boxes and three-ring binders.

He pulled them down in sets, going back for more when the first armload was laid out on the bed. Many of the binders were marked with their respective gaming system. 'Yu-Gi-Oh', 'Pokemon', 'Vampire', 'Magic: the Gathering', 'Munchkin', and more stared up from the bed. Within the cardboard boxes, he pulled out stacks of regular playing cards, Uno cards, and other more obscure games. Joey retrieved board games from beneath the card sets, pulling their cards free from their boxes and adding them to his collection.

Joey set his satchel on the bed and began opening the binders. He pulled cards free seemingly at random and slid them into compartments within the bag. When his satchel was threatening to overflow with cards, Joey snapped shut the outer flap and slung the bag across his chest.

"Hold on, baby," he said to the empty room. "I'm coming for you."

Rushing downstairs, Joey stopped at the couch and pulled a pile of bills from the bank sack. Stuffing them into his pocket, he crossed the living room, pulled open the door, and stepped out into the bright sunlight. As he started down the front steps, he heard sirens from nearby. Looking down the street, a pair of black SUVs roared down the road, their red and blue lights flickering through deeply tinted windows.

Joey knew they were too far away to be heading toward the Montrose building. There was only one reason unmarked black SUVs would be speeding down his street.

Reaching into his bag, he pulled free a few cards from their organized pockets, slipping them underneath his leather bracer.

The SUVs screeched to a halt in front of his building. The doors flew open and men in black suits poured from the vehicle like clowns at the circus. The man leading the group, a dark skinned man whose eyes were lost behind wide aviator sunglasses, approached Joey.

"Joey Scaglione?" he asked sternly.

"Listen, buddy," Joey replied, as he finished walking down his entry steps. "You have really crappy timing. I don't have time for this right now."

"Then make time," the man threatened. When Joey didn't try to push past him, the agent continued. "My name is Agent Mbue and I'm with the Department of Homeland Security. I'd like you to look at a few pictures for me."

Reaching out, one of his agents placed a folder in his hand. Agent Mbue brought the folder back around and opened it before Joey. Inside, a series of pictures were stapled together. The resolution was grainy and features hard to distinguish but Joey didn't need anyone to explain the photos. He saw himself in each picture, standing in front of an ATM. The pictures, he rationalized, were from the ATMs' internal cameras.

"Do you recognize this man?"

Joey frowned. "I'm not an idiot. What do you want?"

Agent Mbue smiled. "Of course you're not. It seems that the man in these photos has been withdrawing money from ATMs across the city, always in quantities of two hundred dollars."

"Is that a crime?" Joey asked, holding up his hands.

"It is when there's absolutely no record of him ever inputting a credit or debit card. I found that funny. Do you find that funny?"

Joey glanced to the downtown skyline, knowing that every second he bickered with the agent was a minute longer that Danica was in trouble. "Sure, it's a freaking riot."

"I took the liberty of running a facial recognition program on you. You know what it said?"

"That I'm a gorgeous man," Joey quipped. "Can we speed this up?"

"It came back and said 'classified'," Agent Mbue responded, unfazed by Joey's sarcasm. "I asked myself why it would say that."

Joey turned back toward the agent angrily. "I have somewhere to be. Arrest me, or get the hell out of my way."

"Who could withdraw money from an ATM without using a card? Who would have a classified sticker over their file? I figured the only right answer is that you're an unregistered Super. So yes, you are under arrest."

Motioning to his agents, the satchel was pulled over

Joey's head and his arms were cuffed behind his back. People stuck their heads out of doors and windows to watch Joey get arrested.

The agents set his satchel on the hood of one of the SUVs and opened the outer flap. Reaching inside, they pulled free handfuls of cards, spreading them over the hood haphazardly.

Joey cringed and sighed. "Can you tell them to please be careful?" he begged.

One of the agents held up a bent card near the bottom of the bag. The orange card was a copy of the one Joey had used on ATMs throughout the city.

"Found it, sir," the agent said, holding it up for Agent Mbue.

"Excellent," Mbue smiled. "Put him in the car."

The SUV sped away as soon as everyone was inside. Joey was alone in the back seat. Agent Mbue held Joey's satchel in his lap while an agent drove hastily through the street

"You're in a lot of trouble, son," Mbue explained as they drove. "There are laws against being unregistered."

"Maybe that's the reason I didn't register," Joey retorted. "Have you ever thought that some of us don't want to be in your database? Have you ever thought that some of us don't want to be heroes?"

Agent Mbue laughed. "If I had even half of your powers, I'd be unstoppable."

The SUV sped through the city, cutting near downtown. Through the thick glass, Joey could hear the cacophony of sirens howling from around the Montrose building. His heart ached at the thought of Danica suffering at the hands of the Puppet Master.

Agent Mbue turned and watched Joey look longingly out the window. Smiling to himself, he motioned toward downtown. "I thought you didn't want to be a hero."

"I don't! I just want to get a friend out of trouble, that's it."

Mbue turned back around flippantly. "Then leave it to the real heroes. The others have Wormhole, so I'm sure they'll teleport back any moment now and stop the Puppet Master."

Joey frowned. Agent Mbue's attitude was exactly the attitude that he despised so much in Belltown. Everyone, even the police and agents, washed their hands of their responsibility to stop criminals, assuming that any real danger would be handled by the random Superhero. When faced with a situation like they were in now, with no heroes to be found, they just couldn't accept that someone else had to step up and save lives.

The SUVs merged onto the freeway. The green sign overhead announced that they would soon be arriving at the airport exit.

"So what now?" Joey asked, as he shifted his weight. He slipped his fingers under the leather bracer. "You take me to jail?"

Mbue laughed. "You're going to jail but not the one you're thinking of."

The sign announcing the airport exit flew past the SUV. Joey slid the first card free from his bracer and concentrated. He could feel the heat on his back as the card started to burn.

As the exit arrived, the driver drove straight past and continued down the freeway.

"What are you doing?" Mbue asked the driver. "That was our exit."

The driver shook his head. "I don't know, sir. I guess I just stopped paying attention for a second there."

Joey released the Uno "Skip Turn" card and let it slide across the seat as he retrieved the next card.

Agent Mbue sniffed the air, smelling the acrid scent of smoke. Shifting his weight, he drew his pistol and spun angrily on Joey.

"What did you do?" he demanded.

The SUV came to a screeching halt on the freeway. The trailing vehicle swerved suddenly to avoid a collision. As they both came to a stop, the doors opened and both the driver and Agent Mbue exited their vehicle. The driver opened Joey's door and helped him out of the SUV. Turning him around, he unlocked the handcuffs, letting them fall to the ground.

Rubbing his wrists to restart the circulation, Joey dropped the "Get Out Of Jail Free" card, its edges curling from the heat.

The other agents jumped from the trailing SUV, their weapons drawn.

"Lower your weapons," Mbue ordered. "We're letting him go."

"We can't do that, sir," the lead agent from the second vehicle replied. "Protocol says you might have been compromised. I need you all to lay down on the ground and place your hands above your heads."

"Sorry," Joey replied flatly. "I can't do that right now."

He held out the last card, barely visible to the advancing men. The Magic: the Gathering card shimmered in the heat. The word "Sleep" was barely visible under the tendrils of smoke.

The agents went limp and dropped heavily onto the freeway. They breathed shallowly as Joey collected their guns and threw them over the side of the overpass.

"Sorry to have to do that to you," he offered the sleeping men. "Hopefully you'll wake up before it gets too hot out here."

Reaching into the front seat of the SUV, Joey pulled out his satchel. He groaned as he opened the lid and saw the disarray within. His precise organization was gone. Hastily, he organized the most important cards back into their pockets before slinging the whole contraption over his shoulder.

In his hands, he retained a single rectangular card. The back was covered with questions meant to stimulate dialogue with young children. Flipping the card over, Joey stared at the "Baby's First Words" card. It never ceased to amaze Joey how every card that depicted a car always showed some version of a sports car.

As he held the card aloft, heat rippled across its surface. Smoke poured from its edges and pooled on the road before him. From the depth of the smoke, a concept sports car appeared in the middle of the freeway. Joey tucked the large rectangular card into his waistband before climbing behind the wheel and speeding away.

CHAPTER EIGHT

The sports car roared to a stop in front of the gaming shop. Joey felt the heat from the 'Baby's First Words' card in his waistband but he ignored the pain and left the car idling on the street.

He heard the familiar ringing of the bell above his head as he pushed through the door. A few customers, flipping through comic books or staring longingly at some of the rarer gaming cards in the display case, looked up as he entered. The owner seemed genuinely surprised to see Joey and smiled at him as he approached.

"You're in here awfully early, aren't you?" he asked jovially.

Joey ignored his pleasantries as he approached the display case. Standing over the cards, he stared lovingly at a card he coveted many times during his frequent visits.

"This one," he said matter-of-factly, pointing at the card at the top of the display. The owner didn't need to see which card he was pointing at, knowing which one he wanted.

"It's..." he began before his mouth went dry. "It's a rare foil edition. It's a hundred and twenty dollars."

Joey reached into his pocket and pulled out a wad of bills. He wasn't sure of the exact amount, but was sure it more than covered the cost of the card.

"Keep the rest for yourself," he said. Pain flared in his back as the car card continued to burn.

The owner smiled broadly. "I'll get it packaged up."

"I don't have time for that. Just give me the card."

The owner pulled out the card and handed it to Joey. As soon as it struck his skin, Joey felt the inherent power concealed just beneath the surface. It represented both his love of the cards and his fear at loving the power they represented.

Dropping it unceremoniously into his satchel, he thanked the owner and rushed out of the store. Smoke trailed behind him from the smoldering card tucked into his jeans.

The sports car approached the police barricade at fast speeds. Joey only applied the brakes when he was dangerously close to the blue wooden sawhorses. No sooner had the car come to a stop than Joey jumped out and pulled the card from his back. The face of the card was nearly black from the internal flames. He dropped it to the ground and the sports car dissipated into mist.

The onlookers gawked at the fading sports car. Without missing a step, Joey withdrew a card and held it up for the crowd to see. They stared intently at the 'Amnesia' card as it scorched from the internal temperature. Slowly, as a mass, they turned away from the street and returned their gaze to the Montrose building.

Pulling a card from his satchel, Joey slid it into the center of his wallet as he approached the police officer. The officer had his back to Joey as he watched the odd puppet standing stoically in front of the Montrose building.

"Excuse me," Joey said to get the man's attention.

The police offer spun suddenly and scowled at Joey.

"This road is closed, sir. You need to leave here immediately, for your own safety."

Joey opened his wallet, revealing the card within. The Vampire card shimmered, blurring the words "FBI Special Affairs Division" across the top.

"Special Agent Mbue," Joey said. "FBI Special Affairs Division."

The police officer stared intently at the card before nodding acceptingly. "What can I do for you, Agent?"

"Special Agent," Joey corrected. "I need to speak to whoever's in charge of the scene." Joey glanced away, trying to look indifferent to the police officer's part of the conversation.

"Captain McHenry is in charge," the officer replied, pointing to a large police mobile command center van. "He's over there."

Joey ducked under the sawhorse. "Thank you, officer."

He walked away hurriedly, before the illusion began to fade in the officer's mind. Despite the card's effectiveness when directly in front of the officer, its power and influence was proportional to its proximity. By the time Joey got to the van, the officer would be questioning exactly what the FBI badge had looked like.

Knocking loudly on the van's door, the door swung open and another officer glared out.

"Who are you and how did you get in here?" he asked gruffly.

"Are you Captain McHenry?"

The officer nodded.

Joey held up the card, risking a second use. Some of its power was already gone, but its influence was still effective.

"Special Agent Michael Hunt," Joey said. "FBI Special Affairs Division."

Captain McHenry squinted at the card. Under scrutiny, the card began to burn in Joey's hand. Sweat broke out on his brow as he suppressed a groan of pain.

"Never heard of them," the Captain replied.

"We're new," Joey lied. "We were created to deal with the Super threat."

For a long moment, Captain McHenry simply stared at Joey. Finally, his stern expression relaxed and he nodded. Knowing the illusion was in place; Joey lowered his wallet and took his finger away from the scalding card.

"What can you tell me about the situation?" Joey asked.

Captain McHenry stepped down from the van and peered around the corner. "The Puppet Master has the place closed up tight. He doesn't seem interested in negotiating. Every entrance has at least one of his puppets standing guard, so there's no way in."

Joey looked around the van and understood the Captain's apprehension. The puppet standing guard at the door was imposing, towering nearly as tall as the lamp posts on either side of the entrance. Scanning to the right, Joey saw a narrow pedestrian bridge arching into the building from a parking structure across the street.

"Where is he now?"

Captain McHenry jerked a thumb skyward. "He's up there on the roof."

Joey covered his brow with his hand, blocking out

the sun as he looked toward the top of the skyscraper. "What's he doing up there?"

"He's just standing there. Our guys think it's because he's using so much power with all the puppets."

Joey frowned. The Puppet Master was far more powerful than the Captain would understand. If he was concentrating, it was for a sinister purpose.

"He's standing out in the open?"

The Captain nodded.

"Why don't you guys just shoot him? Send up a sniper or a helicopter."

Captain McHenry shook his head. "The building is too tall for snipers to get a good shot. We sent up a helicopter already."

Joey didn't like the angry tone in the Captain's voice. Extreme emotions would burn through Joey's illusion even quicker. "What happened?"

"The bastard turned it into a puppet!" McHenry growled. "It opened the doors and kicked out the crew. They dropped nearly four hundred feet, and then it went and joined the Puppet Master on the roof. Like I said earlier, there isn't a way in."

Motioning to the parking structure, Joey turned back to the Captain. "What about that?"

The Captain shook his head. "We tried that. The Puppet Master turned a car into one of his puppets. It killed a couple of my SWAT team before we were able to evacuate."

"Thank you for your time, Captain. I'll be heading that way. I'll let you know as soon as the coast is clear."

The Captain dropped a stern hand on Joey's shoulder. For a moment, Joey feared the effectiveness of the Vampire card had already worn off. The look on the Captain's face, however, was one of concern.

"You're not listening. It killed my men like it was nothing. You'll be killed if you go in there."

Joey patted the Captain's hand before gently removing it from his shoulder. "Well, the Special Affairs Division technically doesn't exist, so you won't have to put anything about my death in your official report."

With a soft smile, Joey walked around the van and jogged toward the parking structure.

CHAPTER NINE

Stepping around the drop-down arm blocking the entrance to the parking structure, Joey stepped into the relative gloom. The main power was out, leaving only the emergency lights glowing intermittently along the ceiling. As the parking structure angled upward, the only separation from the outside was a waist high concrete barrier. Between the top of the barrier and the floor above, sunlight spilled into the structure, illuminating the way.

Joey was sweating and he reflexively dropped his hand into his satchel. The parking garage was full of cars since all the owners were trapped inside the office building. Turning up the first ramp, Joey glanced nervously left and right at the parked cars as he walked. He scolded himself for not asking the Captain the make and model of the puppet car. Instead of looking for a specific type of car, now he was nervously checking every car for sentient murderous intent.

The pedestrian bridge had been three stories up and the walk through the structure was slow going. By now the effect of his last card would be gone, leaving the Captain cursing at the strange civilian who just walked alone into a death trap. Joey didn't envy the Captain's position. Either he would admit that he was fooled by an obviously fake FBI badge and let an unarmed civilian walk into the parking structure, or he would lie and say that someone snuck through his cordon and got themselves killed in the parking structure, showing his incompetence. Neither situation seemed desirable.

At the first landing, Joey found nothing blocking his way. Swinging around the corner, he made his way to the third floor.

As he walked up the gentle incline, he heard the revving of an engine nearby. Joey froze as he searched for the source of the sound. In the concrete garage, the sound echoed at him from all directions. He lifted the top flap of his satchel and found the pocket he wanted, just as he heard the squealing of tires approaching from behind.

Spinning, Joey stared into the head beams of a Corvette as it raced out of its parking spot and launched directly at him. Despite the blinding high beams shining in his eyes, Joey could tell that no one sat behind the wheel.

Dropping to his knee, Joey pulled out the card and held it protectively in front of his face. He closed his eyes tightly, not wanting to see the car hurtling toward him. The Corvette locked its breaks at the last moment, sending smoke billowing from its tires and it slid to a stop. Opening one eye, Joey stared at the grill of the sports car stopped only a few feet from him.

Immediately, the area behind the Corvette illuminated by its reverse lights. The car raced back down the ramp, not bothering to apply its breaks as it slid back into its parking spot and slammed into the concrete barrier with enough force to shatter it. The Corvette passed through the barrier and fell over the edge of the parking structure, flipping as it fell. It struck the ground upside down, smashing in the roof and hood. For a brief moment, its tires spun as it sought traction.

As the spinning tires stopped, the head lights dimmed and went out.

Letting out a sigh of relief, Joey dropped the Uno 'Reverse' card. Jogging up the rest of the ramp toward the pedestrian causeway, Joey caught himself frowning. Everything so far had been deliberately planned in advance. He knew which cards he would need and had them prepared before putting himself in harm's way. From this point on, he would have to rely on his reflexes, quick thinking, and his card organization.

At least he was confident that his cards were in order.

CHAPTER TEN

As he approached the pedestrian bridge, the doors in front of him swung slowly open. Under normal circumstances, Joey wouldn't have given a second thought to the automatically opening doors. Glancing at the frame of the door, however, he frowned after realizing that it wasn't an automatic door. The Puppet Master knew he was coming and was inviting him inside. That made a knot tighten in his gut. The element of surprise was his best weapon when going up against another Super.

Knowing he had few other options, Joey stepped through the door. They swung shut quickly behind him and he heard the telltale clicking of the locking mechanism.

Sunlight streamed through the intermittently spaced windows running the length of the hall. The carpeted floor beneath his feet silenced his steps but Joey wasn't fooled enough to think he could sneak up on the Puppet Master anymore. His only hope now was to avoid as many of his puppets as possible on his way to the rooftop.

At the far end of the hallway, assorted furniture was stacked against the interior doorway, effectively blocking his way into the Montrose building. A large office desk was tilted on its side, sharing the space with a silver refrigerator. Other smaller pieces of furniture were stacked into the open spaces between the larger objects. From the opposite end of the hall, Joey could see an office chair, coffee pot, and filing cabinet dropped haphazardly around the legs of the table.

"You can come on out," Joey shouted into the hall. He fumbled with the pockets of his satchel, searching for cards that would help. "I know you're there."

For a moment, nothing happened. Like a bear waking from its hibernation, the stack of furniture shook itself as it tried to untangle from one another. The lower drawers of the refrigerator reached downward, pushing its bulk off of the floor. The double doors swung outward and bent at their tips, reaching down like hooks.

The table bent its back legs and lowered itself down until all four legs were comfortably on the ground. It scurried a few feet forward like a crab before rocking back on its rear legs and swinging its front feet like massive clubs.

Joey could barely make out the other pieces of furniture, but could smell the faint scent of burning carpet and had to assume the coffee maker was heating its internal coils.

"All right, Puppet Master," Joey muttered. "You know I'm here. So you want to play rough? We'll play rough."

Slipping his fingers into the 'Vampire: the Eternal Struggle' cards, Joey withdrew a pair and held them in the open palm of his hand.

"Come get some," he said, feeling every bit the Superhero.

As the table scuttled toward him, Joey pulled the first card, which immediately ignited with internal flames. The words 'Acrobatics' smoked and turned black, consumed by the bubbling heat.

Running forward, he met the desk halfway down the hall. Joey hurdled the desk easily, his fingers barely touching the tabletop as he tucked his knees underneath him.

Instead of landing on his feet, Joey dropped to his knees and rolled forward. A drawer from the filing cabinet flew inches above his head, launched like an arrow down the hall. Ending his roll, he extended a foot and drove his heel into the coffee machine as it approached. The coffee maker shattered, its red coils instantly cooling as it lost its sentience.

Raising his knees, Joey pushed himself straight upward in a kip up, his back barely clearing the swinging wooden club of the office table. Landing on his feet, Joey drew the second card and threw it downward. Flying straight, the tip of the card pierced the carpet and stuck upright.

Over the words 'Time Bomb', a faint red number five appeared. As Joey began running forward again, the five faded away and a red four took its place.

Slipping to the side, Joey avoided a second filing cabinet drawer. The office chair hurtled toward him, rolling along the carpeted floor. Joey leapt into the seat, driving his knees into the backrest. His momentum drove the chair backward, rolling it into the final oncoming drawer. The drawer smashed across its back and the squirming armrests of the chair went limp.

Behind him, the four faded to a three.

The refrigerator moved forward angrily, waving its outstretched arms like scythes. In midstride, Joey ran to his right and planted his foot on the wall. His momentum took him up the wall a few steps before he was able to flip from the wall. He landed behind the refrigerator, who struggled sluggishly to turn around. Its bulk blocked the table as well, which shifted from side to side in the hallway.

Reaching the far door, Joey glanced at the empty filing cabinet, which seemed to shrink from his glare.

Turning toward the table and refrigerator, Joey held up his pointer and middle fingers, as the Time Bomb card showed a red number two. As the two faded to a one, Joey dropped his pointer finger and turned his middle finger to the approaching furniture.

The explosion that followed sheared the center of the pedestrian bridge, dropping flaming rubble into the street below. Caught in the blast, the table and refrigerator disappeared in the ball of fire before falling into the chasm.

Beneath his feet, the ground shook violently. Joey braced himself against the doorframe as he felt cracks extend beneath the carpet, reaching to his feet. For a second, he feared the card had been too strong and the entire bridge would collapse. Eventually, the shaking subsided, leaving Joey standing at the edge of the shattered vestibule.

Beside him, the filing cabinet turned its empty face toward Joey curiously. Reaching over, Joey gave it a shove, dropping it into the open maw beyond his feet. The filing cabinet shattered into twisted metal when it struck the asphalt three stories below.

Checking the door behind him, Joey found it unlocked. Reaching into his satchel, he reached into the nearly empty 'Super Munchkin' pocket, drawing the single card within. Holding the Invisibility card close to his chest, he faded from view.

Joey walked into the lobby beyond the door and quickly slipped against the wall. An odd assortment of puppets shuffled past him, responding to the explosion and loss of their counterparts. Quietly, Joey let them pass and entered deeper into the building.

Around the corner from the lobby, he saw the illuminated exit sign, pointing to a nearby stairwell. Glancing over his shoulder, he made sure nothing was looking in his direction before pushing open the door and slipping inside the staircase.

In front of him, a large white three was written on the gray wall. Tilting his head upward, he looked at the vertigo-inducing tower of stairs ahead of him. Danica's office was located over thirty floors above him.

Frowning, Joey opened his satchel and flipped through his remaining cards. Angrily, he flipped the lid closed again and raised his eyes back to the pillar of stairs above him.

"All the cards I brought," Joey lamented, "and I didn't think to bring a single 'flight' or 'teleportation' card. Dumbass."

Sighing, he began hurrying up the first of thirty-six flights of stairs.

CHAPTER ELEVEN

Joey pulled hard on the stairwell railing, dragging himself onto the next landing. The large white numbers next to the doorway read thirty-eight. Leaning forward, he placed his hands on his knees and tried to catch his breath. Doubled over, he turned and looked at the next flight of stairs. Shuffling forward, he placed a heavy foot onto the first step and groaned as he began to climb the stairs.

At the landing for floor thirty-nine, Joey sat down and leaned back against the wall. Closing his eyes, he tried to listen beyond the closed door for any telltale scuffling of the Puppet Master's creations. Instead, all he heard was the crashing crescendo of blood rushing past his ears.

Reaching over, he flipped open the flap of his satchel and took inventory of the cards remaining. His trip to the stairwell used a majority of his normal cards. Those that remained represented a dangerous part of Joey's powers: monsters. Creatures that card gamers craved for their savagery were far more disturbing when brought to life. A vampire was alluring when staring up from a card with burning, dead eyes. In actuality, those dead eyes were cold and haunting and left Joey feeling like maggots were crawling under his skin.

Flipping the lid of the bag closed again, Joey pushed himself upright and walked to the doorway. Placing his hand on the door handle, he took a deep breath and turned the knob.

The staircase emerged halfway down a hallway. The overhead lights still illuminated the hall in both directions. The carpet before the door was torn and Joey was able to trace the scraped fabric as far as he could see in both directions. Something large, one of the puppets no doubt, had paced past this door innumerable times on a calculated patrol of the floor.

Glancing back and forth, Joey hoped the puppet stayed on the far side of the building. It wouldn't take him long to reach Danica's office but he couldn't risk encountering such a large puppet. Joey had a few more tricks up his sleeve – both figuratively and literally – but fighting the puppet would leave him even more depleted.

Slipping into the hallway, he rushed as quietly as possible down the hall. Pausing at every corner, he scanned for signs of the shambling puppet. Taking turns like a twisting maze, Joey eventually found himself outside a wooden double door. Around its rim, small, square frosted windows rimmed the doorframe.

Placing his hands against the glass to block out the glare, Joey lowered his face toward the frosted panes. Beyond, he could barely make out blurry shapes, silhouetted against the sunlight pouring through the office windows. Walking to the center of the doors, he pushed on the handles to no avail. Both doors were locked tightly.

Glancing nervously over his shoulder, Joey slid his satchel over his shoulder and set it on the ground in front of him. Working quickly, he flipped open the lid and began sorting through the cards within. Each pocket turned up nothing of value. Swearing quietly, he pulled out a single card and swung the bag back over his head.

Of all the cards in his repertoire, none had offered a means to unlock the door without violence.

Glancing down at the card in his hand, he knew that he had chosen the least disturbing of all the monster cards in his arsenal. Hoping the comical depiction on the card would help alleviate most of his concerns, he gripped the card tightly in his hand.

Leaning forward, Joey pressed his mouth against the crack between the doors.

"Danica," he hissed as loud as he dared. Joey immediately glanced down the hall, making sure nothing had been alerted. "Danica, it's Joey. I'm here to get you out. If you can hear me, I need you to stay away from the door. You hear me? Stay away from the door."

Backing up to the far wall, Joey glanced down at the card and scowled.

"Here goes nothing," he muttered. He turned the card so it faced the doorway. "I choose you."

The edges of the card browned and curled. Thick white smoke billowed from the card and fell to the ground in dense waves. As it settled onto the floor, it began to coalesce between Joey and the door. From its amorphous shape, it began to form into the vague shape of the canine.

The gray smoke gave way to wiry orange fur. A stunted tail wagged furiously as it turned solid. Three of its stocky legs stood on the ground. Each leg ended in two toes and an opposable thumb, which it used to pinch at the carpeted floor.

Joey felt nauseous as the rest of the canine took shape. A ridged spine developed from the base of the tail. Powerful shoulders emerged from the smoke, leading into a taunt neck. As the head took shape, it was readily apparent that it was far too large for the small dog. Resting over the normal head of the creature, a cow skull was affixed. It moved easily with the creature as it shook its head from side to side. Turning its head toward him, Joey saw the beady black eyes staring at him exuberantly from beneath the hollow eye sockets of the skull.

Turning its head also revealed the fourth arm, which it held aloft. Firmly grasped between its fingers and opposable thumb, the canine clung to a white femur. Sharp teeth marks marred the surface. Groaning, Joey prayed the bone wasn't a human's.

"You're a disgusting little freak, you know that, Cubone?" Joey asked, looking down at the demonic, orange Jack Russell Terrier.

Cubone yipped softly and wagged its tale feverishly.

"Alright, you cannibalistic mutt. You think you can head butt your way through that door?"

The dog turned toward the door and growled. Lowering its head, it exposed the heavily polished surface of the skull, angling it toward the center of the doorway.

"Go get it, boy," Joey encouraged.

Cubone sprung forward, all four of its feet leaving the ground simultaneously. It launched forward like a bullet, striking the door with its head. The hard wood of the door shattered from the impact, spraying the room beyond with broken slivers.

As Cubone passed through the door, Joey released the card in disgust. Intermixed with the splinters, Cubone lost shape and evaporated into mist. Dropping the card onto the carpeted floor, he wiped his hands on his jeans, feeling suddenly unclean.

Hurrying through the broken doorway, Joey glanced into the nearby offices.

"Danica," he said loudly, as it was no longer necessary to remain quiet. His plan had previously been to sneak through the building and save his girlfriend. With stealth no longer an option, he was going to have to rely on speed.

"Danica," he called again.

A figure stepped into one of the doorways and Joey's hand fell reflexively to the satchel on his hip. He released his grip quickly as he recognized the frightened figure.

"Joey?" Danica asked, disbelief evident in her voice.

"I'm here, baby," he said softly.

Danica rushed to him and he enveloped her in his arms. Joey held her tight as sobs wracked her body. He buried his head in her hair, kissing her softly on top of her head.

"I'm here, Danica, I'm here."

"I knew you'd come for me," she cried.

Joey slid his hands to Danica's arms and gently pushed her back. She stared up at him with concern, but he smiled disarmingly.

"We can't stay here, baby. There's a puppet on this floor and I know it heard me bust through the door. We need to go now."

Danica nodded but quickly began shaking her head. "What about the others?"

Joey looked over her shoulder. "Who else is in the office?"

"Not in the office, Joey," she replied sternly. "Everyone ran out as soon as the Puppet Master showed up. I don't know where they wound up. I'm talking about everyone else in the building."

Joey pressed his lips into a bloodless line. "I don't give a crap about the rest of the building. I came for you."

"You can't just leave them," she replied, pushing herself out of his grip. "Who knows what the Puppet Master will do to them if you don't save them."

Joey glanced over his shoulder at the empty hallway beyond. Turning back to Danica, he scowled.

"What do you expect me to do? Do you have any idea how many puppets are running around this building?"

"What do I expect you to do? I expect you to be a hero!"

"Can we not have this conversation right now? Anyways, take a look around. In case you didn't notice, I am being a freaking hero! I came for you, didn't I?"

Danica crossed her arms over her chest. "Being a hero is about more than saving the people you know. It's about saving the people you don't know! It's about doing the right thing when no one's watching and when no one expects it!"

"Jesus Christ," Joey muttered. "You're not going to be happy until I go up and face the Puppet Master, are you?"

Danica smiled softly and placed her hand on his chest. "You can do it, Joey. You're so much stronger than you think you are."

Joey sighed, knowing he was losing both the battle

and the war. His frown deepened as he realized that facing the Puppet Master might also result in him losing his life.

"Can we get you to safety first? Will you let me do that before I worry about the other thousand people around here?"

Danica leaned forward and kissed him. "I knew you had it in you."

Slipping her hand in his, they turned toward the doorway. As they took a step forward, an enormous shadow fell over the hallway. Wooden legs tore at the fabric of the carpet as an antique wardrobe turned and blocked the exit.

When it opened its doors, Danica cringed at the sharpened coat hooks that glistened like shark's teeth from its interior. Raising a hand to her mouth, she suppressed a scream.

Joey felt anger bubble within him. He was already far too tired of the Puppet Masters automatons.

Stuffing his hand into his satchel, Joey pulled out a hexagon card and held it toward the wardrobe.

"Settlers of Catan," Joey spat. "Wood, bitch!"

A massive, sharpened log launched from the card like a ballistae. The wardrobe tried to close its doors defensively but the log shattered the doors and pierced through the core of the piece of furniture. The back of the wardrobe exploded as the lumber pinned it to the wall. It twitched like a skewered insect before reverting to a normal wardrobe.

"Wow!" Danica yelped. "That was incredible!"

Joey turned toward her, his face flush with excitement. "Can I leave you here for a little bit?"

Danica understood and nodded with a smile. "Go get him, darling."

Joey kissed her deeply before walking to the doorway.

"Go back and hide in one of the offices," he said. "I'll come back for you when I'm done. No matter what happens, don't panic."

She nodded and rushed back to her office.

"I love you," he called after her.

Danica turned with a smile. "I love you too, sweetie."

"Baby?" he said as she retreated.

"Yes?"

Joey pulled a card from his pack. Holding up the trivial pursuit card, he read the question. "What happened in New York on November 9, 1965?"

"I don't know," she replied with a broad grin.

"A blackout," Joey said, returning her smile.

All the lights in the building, including the emergency lights, went out simultaneously.

Stepping into the enveloping darkness of the hallway, Joey fingered the other card in his hand. A small shimmer of red rolled over the card, briefly illuminating the picture of the night vision goggles.

Lowering the goggles over his eyes, the world erupted into shades of green. Joey walked to a second stairwell under the cover of darkness. The interior stairwell, unlike the one on which he began, offered roof access.

Opening the door softly, he scanned both up and down the stairs. Gratefully, the roof was only a few floors above. Reverberating off the concrete walls, Joey could plainly hear the pair of puppets shuffling back and forth at the entrance to the roof.

Climbing a few floors as quietly as possible, Joey glanced upward again. With the augmented night vision, he could see the surprisingly human expressions of the two puppet office tables who were staring over the railing. Cast in the complete darkness of the stairwell, they were glancing around blindly.

Continuing quietly forward, Joey climbed the stairs until he reached the midpoint landing, just one set of stairs below the puppets. They stepped back and forth on the narrow landing in front of the rooftop access door, repeatedly running into one another in their blindness. He reached into his bag and withdrew a card from one of the front most pockets. Glancing down, he felt the hollow in the pit of his stomach growing even larger.

The snarling face of an orc stared up from the surface of the 'Magic: the Gathering' card. Ferocious, the green-skinned monster was frozen in the middle of swinging a wickedly crafted axe.

Taking a knee, Joey concentrated on the card. The quick shimmer of light alerted the puppets moments before the orc leapt from the card. It snarled as it flexed its heavily tattooed arms. Lifting its axe above its head, the orc let loose a battle yell.

One of the puppets reached behind it and pushed open the door, bathing the stairwell in bright sunlight. Joey cringed as his night vision goggled were overwhelmed and went brilliant white. Pulling them off his face, Joey couldn't see his monster. Seeing it was unnecessary as he heard it charging up the stairs. A loud crash echoed through the stairwell as the Orc and puppets crashed through the open doorway in a jumbled heap.

The dancing spots in Joey's vision faded to blue and black. Blinking away the spots, he rubbed his eyes and pushed himself to his feet. Knowing what was beyond the open doorway, his heart began to pound in his chest. Taking a deep breath, he climbed the last set of stairs.

Laying on the rooftop beyond the door, thick smoke mingled between the broken remnants of two tables. Clearly visible axe marks marred the wooden surfaces.

Stepping into the bright sunlight, Joey stared across the roof at the black-garbed man standing with his back to him. Pushing through the broken debris, Joey approached the man slowly.

Turning toward him, the Puppet Master pushed back his cloak theatrically, exposing the assortment of black clothing beneath. Over his face, an unfinished wooden puppet's mask sat. Its light brown wooden texture accentuated the comically bulbous nose and rounded cheeks. Where the blockish mouth of a marionette was normally found, it was absent, revealing the Puppet Master's own mouth and chin beneath.

"Who dares challenge the Puppet Master?" he yelled, his voice rolling over the rooftop. "Do you not realize who I am? Only a fool would…"

The Puppet Master stopped and stared at Joey. They were a bizarre pair, facing one another across the rooftop of a forty-story office building. The Puppet Master had clearly embraced his dramatic villain role, while Joey wore the same clothes he had worn to a poker game the night before.

Reaching up, the Puppet Master pushed his mask off his face, letting it rest on top his head. The handsome features underneath were a far departure from the cartoonish wooden mask.

"Joey?" the Puppet Master asked in disbelief.

"Hi, Greg."

CHAPTER TWELVE

The Puppet Master embraced Joey, patting him strongly on the back. He let out a surprised laugh as he stepped back and held Joey at arm's reach.

"I can't believe it's really you!" Greg exclaimed. "I haven't seen you in, what, eight years?"

Joey smiled weakly. He shoved his hands in his pockets and glanced around the rooftop. "Not since the end of the war."

"Yet here you are." The Puppet Master released Joey and placed his hands on his hips. His handsome face was split with a broad grin. "What have you been up to all this time?"

"Not a whole lot really. I've been trying my best to live a normal life and just kind of forget about everything that happened during the war."

"No kidding," the Puppet Master said soberly. "Are you still playing cards?"

Joey smiled for once, recalling his most recent misadventures during a poker game. "Still playing cards."

"Man, we couldn't go anywhere without you busting out a deck of cards and trying to take all our money."

"That's still pretty much what I do now."

Greg smacked Joey on the arm. "I can't believe you're here after all this time. Last time I got together with some of the others, we were talking about the people we haven't heard from in a while. I don't remember who it was that brought up your name, but someone asked about you. Of course, none of us had seen you in forever."

Glancing over Joey's shoulder, the Puppet Master eyed the remains of his two puppets, smashed on the rooftop.

"How did you even get up here? You would have had to make your past a dozen puppets at least. Wait, was that you taking out all my puppets?"

Joey shrugged.

"How? When we redeployed, you didn't have any powers."

"I did, apparently. I just hadn't figured out what it was at the time."

"Can you show me?"

Joey reached into his satchel and withdrew a 'Magic: the Gathering' card. In the picture window on the card, an innocuous Goblin stared at the pair of men.

Concentrating, Joey felt the card heat between his fingers. From the picture window a hand emerged, grasping the frame of the card. The Goblin pushed itself free, hopping the few inches to the ground. At full height, the Goblin was barely taller than two and a half feet. Its oversized head balanced precariously on its thin green body. In its hand, the Goblin wielded a jagged bone knife, which it jabbed into the open air before it. With every stab, the monster cackled with a sadistic glee.

"That is so cool," Greg laughed. "At least I know how you made it through my puppets."

With a wave of his hand, Joey fanned the Goblin with its card. The wind blew through the Goblin, causing it to lose consistency. It evaporated with each pass of the card, leaving behind a fading fog.

The Puppet Master looked up from the dissipating creature and locked eyes with Joey. "What are you actually doing here, though? Why go through all the effort to destroy my puppets?"

Joey looked away, embarrassed. "I'm…God, this sounds so dumb. I'm here to stop you."

Greg laughed at his old friend. His laugh faded as he noticed the smile missing from Joey's face. "You're not serious, are you? Why now?"

"You kidnapped my girlfriend. She works in this building."

Greg threw his arms out to his side. "Is that it? Man, I'm sorry. You have to know that I had no idea your girlfriend worked here. Please, take her and get her to safety. I'll make sure all my puppets stay out of your way."

"What about the other nine hundred and ninety-nine people in the building? What are you going to do with them?"

Greg furrowed his brow. "They're my hostages, Joey. They're what are keeping the police at bay. Where are you going with this?"

"Greg, you can't do this. You have innocent hostages. Hell, you killed an entire helicopter crew!"

"Of course I did! They were trying to kill me!"

Joey flushed with frustration. "They were trying to kill you because you took a thousand hostages, you idiot! You can't use one crime to justify another!"

Greg grew suddenly quiet. "So that's it? I don't see you for eight years and this is how we're going to reunite? You're just going to show up while I'm working and decide to suddenly play the hero?"

"I don't want to play the hero but you're not leaving me a lot of options," Joey replied sadly.

"Just walk away from this while you still can," Greg replied dangerously.

"I want to, believe me, but I can't. I can't just let you do this to all these people. If the other Supers were around, I wouldn't be here at all. But with them gone, someone has to stand up to you."

The Puppet Master smiled wickedly as he lowered his wooden mask back over his face. "You were never a hero, Joey. I'm guessing you don't even have much experience playing the hero. I've been doing this for the past eight years. Do you really think you stand a chance against me?"

Joey dropped his hand into his bag. "I guess we'll find out."

Drawing out two cards simultaneously, he held them in front of his face. Smoke billowed from both as the ink on their surfaces bubbled. From out of the smoke, a stocky dwarf and another brutal orc emerged.

"Give up, Greg. I don't want to have to do this."

Joey could see the thin smile from beneath Greg's mask. "There is no more 'Greg'. Only the Puppet Master remains."

The clang of metal sounded from behind the staircase. Backing away, Joey's jaw dropped as the helicopter stepped around the corner. Its tail fin was split into a pair of legs, while the side doors were transformed into arms. The Plexiglas windshield was tilted upward, giving the illusion of a head mounted atop the monstrous contraption.

Reaching behind it, the helicopter detached its rotor blades. Gripping the four blades in front of it, the puppet nimbly spun them in its hand until their movement was a mere blur.

Advancing in ringing, stuttered steps, the helicopter descended on Joey's two creations.

The dwarf raised his hammer and charged the machine. With a swipe of its blades, the puppet cut through the stocky figure. The dwarf lost its solidity and faded to mist as the blades passed through its body.

Releasing an angry battle cry, the orc raised its axe over its head and threw it toward the puppet. The metal axe clanged harmlessly off the helicopter's protective undercarriage. The orc looked disbelievingly as the puppet turned on him. Like the dwarf before him, the orc was obliterated with a swipe of its rotor.

"Give this up, Joey!" The Puppet Master demanded from his place near the edge of the roof. "You can't hope to defeat me."

"I'm not done yet," Joey replied.

Withdrawing a handful of cards, Joey began summoning one after another. Before him, Orcs appeared next to Ogres. Vampires stood shoulder-to-shoulder with Pokemon. Werewolves stood defiantly with Elves.

Undeterred, the helicopter advanced on them all. Joey's creatures launched volleys of arrows and javelins at the puppet, but they had no effect on the automaton. Sweeping its blades in wide arcs, the puppet cut through his minions as quickly as he could create more.

Stepping back, Joey drew another set of cards. Holding up the top most card from the stack, he concentrated again. A deafening roar erupted from the card moments before an ogre appeared on the roof. Standing nearly as tall as the helicopter, the ogre was a disturbing series of bulbous muscles. Hefting a massive club, the ogre stomped toward the helicopter.

The lesser creatures scattered before the ogre, not willing to be in the way of either its massive feet or gigantic tree trunk.

Cutting down a vampire, the puppet turned just as the ogre swung its club. The heavy wood crashed into the helicopter, shattering its shoulder. Staggering, the puppet struggled to maintain its balance as the ogre readied itself for another swing.

Glancing past the dueling monstrosities, Joey watched the Puppet Master standing impassively. His arms hung limply at his side as he lost himself in deep concentration. Joey frowned, knowing that Greg didn't require much concentration to maintain the number of puppets currently in the building. Even managing the combat wouldn't have taken all Greg's attention. Something was amiss.

From the rooftop doorway, more puppets poured onto the roof. Drawn from throughout the building, an amalgamation of furniture charged into Joey's mass of creatures.

Furniture shattered and fell to the rooftop, which was lost in a swirling sea of thick smoke.

The ogre howled in pain as an office chair drove a letter opener into its exposed calf. Angrily, it swung its club downward, smashing the chair against the roof. Distracted by the chair, the ogre exposed itself to the helicopter. Driving its blade forward like a lance, the puppet pierced the ogre's chest. The ogre gurgled and looked down in confusion, moments before he lost his form.

Looking past the ogre, the helicopter noticed Joey reaching for more cards from his depleted satchel. Covering the rooftop in a few strides, the helicopter charged his position.

Noticing its approach, Joey panicked and fumbled with the cards in his hand. Despite having a handful of monsters, he couldn't concentrate enough to bring one to life. As the roof shook from its advancing footsteps, Joey's hands grew slick with sweat and the cards fell from his shaking fingers.

Looking up with pleading eyes, he watched the helicopter cover the last of the ground between them. Raising its blades above its head, it slashed at an angle, cutting into Joey's chest.

He screamed in pain as the blades cut a wicked gash in his skin. Their metal edges cut through his jacket and shirt and bit into the flesh beneath. Blood splattered onto the roof, spilling from the ugly wound.

Gasping for breath, Joey tumbled backward and collapsed onto the hot roof. With his concentration gone, his creations lost substance and dissipated. Pressing a hand futilely against the bloody cut, Joey groaned in anguish.

The Puppet Master didn't offer him even a cursory glance as his helicopter stalked away from the bleeding man. His other puppets settled around Greg defensively as Joey lay on the ground in pain.

Reaching to his hip, Joey noticed that his satchel was gone. He located it a few feet away, its over-the-shoulder strap severed by the helicopter's blades. Tears forming in his eyes, he dragged himself toward the bag, leaving a smear of blood in his wake.

With shaking hands, he pushed aside the top flap and glanced inside. Spots danced in his vision, making it hard to concentrate on the cards within. Closing his eyes, he let his fingers walk through the pockets until he was certain he found the card he sought.

Drawing the card, Joey tried to block out the pain and just concentrate on activating the card. For a dangerously long second, nothing happened. Biting his lip, he drew together as much focus as he could muster and tried again. Slowly, the card heated in his hand.

Opening his eyes slowly, he stared at the 'Regeneration' card in his hand. Immediately, tendrils of flesh and muscle spanned the breadth of the gash on his chest, drawing the two walls of the injury together. The skin pulled together and sealed until his chest was whole again, without so much as a scar to mark his grave injury.

The color returned to his face and his breathing stabilized.

"You want to make this personal?" he muttered. "We'll make this personal."

Slipping his hand back into the bag, Joey withdrew his newly purchased card. Breaking the seal on the sides of the special display case, he carefully withdrew the card as he pushed himself to his feet.

CHAPTER THIRTEEN

Barely visible amidst the shifting mass of puppets surrounding him, the Puppet Master kept his head lowered and eyes closed. None of the puppets reacted when Joey stood and walked toward the center of the rooftop. Even the robotic helicopter, one arm hanging limply by wires from its shattered shoulder, ignored the diminutive man.

"We're not done here, Greg!" Joey yelled.

As one, the puppet turned toward the angry Italian. Sinking toward the ground, the puppets cleared the Puppet Master's line of vision so he could stare at his old friend.

"You're committed to this hero business," Greg called across the expanse. "I'll give you that. The problem with you hero types is that you don't know when to quit. Let me give you a hint: now is that time."

The helicopter lifted its rotor blades and began idly spinning them in his hand. Joey cringed, knowing how dangerous they could be. His regeneration trick couldn't be repeated, which meant another gash from the blades would be fatal.

"I'll give you a chance to give this up," Joey retorted. "Don't make me stop you."

Greg laughed in disbelief. "You just don't get it, do you? What trick are you going to pull out of your sleeve that I can't immediately counter? Take a look around, Joey. You're outnumbered and outgunned. Face it, you're done!"

"I'm not done. Hell, you haven't seen anything yet."

The hair on Joey's arm stood on end, as though the card in his hand held its own electrical charge. In his chest, his heart fluttered with anticipation as he held the card aloft.

In the cracks between the roof tiles, the mortar began to bubble. The heat rolled across Joey's face in waves, causing sweat to bead across his brow. In the center of the furnace, he felt like an ant underneath an enormous magnifying glass.

His hands shook as he focused on his summon. From the boiling mortar, waves of dancing haze stretched high over his head. The haze hung like a curtain; a backdrop framing Joey as his hair whipped wildly in the localized wind.

Nervously, the Puppet Master sent in a few of his puppets to stop Joey. As they reached the boiling rooftop, their wooden appendages burst into flame. They recoiled in horror as the flames quickly spread and consumed the creations.

Through the curtain, the sunny blue sky turned dark and ominous. Storm clouds roiled as lightning crashed between their bulbous masses. As Joey struggled to hold onto the card, he felt his power suddenly surge. It poured through him like a conduit, feeding the haze behind him.

A giant claw pierced the curtain, emerging above Joey's head and casting him into a deep shadow. The claw reached past him and crashed down onto the rooftop. A deafening roar broke through the air as a second claw emerged. The claws were covered in sparkling silver scales that reflected Joey's image a hundred times in its multifaceted surfaces.

Finally breaking into their world, the dragon's head emerged from the haze. The long, silvery neck ended in a bullet shaped head. Opening its mouth in another screeching roar, it exposed row after row of razor sharp teeth.

The rest of its body emerged, covering the entire back quarter of the expansive rooftop. It spread its leathery wings wide, dipping their tips over either edge of the building.

The Puppet Master stepped back, mortified at the giant monstrosity before him. Closing his eyes again, Greg concentrated as his smaller puppets surged forward.

With a swipe of a clawed hand, the 'Blue-Eyes White Dragon' destroyed the first wave of animated office furniture. Bringing around its tail, it swept a handful of the creations over the edge of the roof. They fell wordlessly to the ground nearly forty stories beneath them.

Around the rooftop, other inanimate objects came to life. The industrial air conditioning unit pulled its fan blades free in a miniaturized mockery of the helicopter puppet. Satellite dishes stood on narrow legs and held antennas aloft like javelins and lances.

Undeterred, Joey clung to the burning 'Yu-Gi-Oh' card in his hand. He could feel the skin on his fingers burning away under the assault, but he refused to release his last and most powerful weapon.

As the rooftop filled with new puppets, Joey smiled wickedly.

"Blue-Eyes White Dragon," he yelled, in imitation

of the cartoon characters that spawned his newest card, "why don't we show them what you can do. Give them 'White Lightening'!"

The dragon opened its mouth as widely as it could. In the center of its soft pink mouth, a ball of blinding white light formed. Swirling madly, the ball picked up speed as it grew in size.

Joey felt electrified as sparks crackled from the ball, drawn outward toward the dragon's impenetrable silver skin.

The air itself felt irrevocably drawn toward the dragon's open maw. The ball grew even larger, now towering over Joey and the majority of puppets. The Puppet Master's creations stuttered forward hesitantly, unsure of whether or not to proceed toward the ominous dragon. Sliding toward the edge of the roof, Greg kept his eyes closed, deep in concentration.

The air was drawn from the Joey's lungs as the air pressure around him became unbearable. When he felt on the cusp of passing out, the 'Blue-Eyes White Dragon' released a roar that shook the rooftop and released its beam of heavenly power.

The blast rocketed from its mouth, tearing through the puppets and rooftop alike. The lesser puppets were obliterated instantly. The helicopter threw up its hands defensively in front of its face as the beam struck him. The Plexiglas melted, running over its metal body. The fragile hinges holding its limbs in place cracked and exploded under the intense heat. As the blast focused on the helicopter, the puppet crumbled to the ground in smoldering pieces.

With the puppets destroyed, the 'White Lightening'

attack dwindled away. Despite the midday sun burning overhead, the world seemed remarkably darker without the blinding beam's presence.

In the aftermath of the blast, Joey took in the destruction before him. The center of the rooftop was gouged, exposing the floor beneath. The edges of the destruction glowed a dangerous red and white as the seared tiles cooled quickly in the blowing breeze. Joey's corner of the roof remained unscathed, as did the area around the Puppet Master. As much as he wanted to stop his old comrade, Joey had no desire to see him dead.

"It's over, Greg," Joey called, as he caught his breath. He felt exhausted with the exertion of keeping the dragon substantial. "You have nothing left."

"On the contrary," the Puppet Master replied confidently. "While you kept yourself busy with lesser minions, I was able to finish what I came here to do."

The ground beneath Joey's feet lurched, throwing him to the rooftop. Rolling onto his back, he stared in horror as the bricks of the building disassembled and reassembled into a gigantic arm, dwarfing even his dragon. The building itself, the Puppet Master's newest puppet, reached down and clamped enormous fingers over the 'Blue-Eyes White Dragon's' neck and back.

Joey cursed himself loudly. Since first being told about Greg's concentration on the roof, he knew it didn't take him that much focus to control his army of puppets. Joey had always suspected Greg was up to more than the police believed but he let his confidence overwhelm his common sense when it came time to face his nemesis.

The hand clamped tighter around the dragon, which

howled in pain. The silver skin crumpled under the devastating fingers as it squeezed the life from Joey's creation.

There hadn't been a time, until very recently, that Joey had considered himself truly a Super. His power seemed inconsequential compared to the others, the Puppet Master included. It had been his own foolishness that had convinced him otherwise; an insufferable male ego that was wounded by his girlfriend's repeated doubts. As he watched the wings collapse, broken beneath the animated building, Joey frowned. Everything he believed about the moral ambivalence of those who waited for Superheroes to save the day was founded. The police stood no chance of defeating a forty-story tall puppet. Only someone powerful like Strong Man or Inferno could save the day. It's what they did. Saving the day was where they excelled.

Looking over his shoulder, he saw the apparent glee on the Puppet Master's masked face. So long as Superheroes existed, it seemed inevitable that Supervillains like the Puppet Master, Razor, or Gust would exist as well. It was a violent cycle that drew the rest of the world into its devastating web.

Knowing his cause was lost, Joey released the card in his hand. With a final howl, the dragon erupted into dense smoke, which settled over the rooftop and poured through the gouge in the tiles.

Pushing himself to his feet, Joey eyed his satchel as it emerged through the sinking mist. As his eyes fell upon it, the Puppet Master saw it as well. The roof beneath it opened like a hungry maw and swallowed it whole. As the leather strap disappeared beneath the tiles, they slammed shut. Defeated, Joey stared after the vanished satchel with his remaining cards.

"Now it's over," Greg called.

The Puppet Master walked around the edge of the building until he and Joey were standing on the same unmarred island of rooftop.

"You could have killed me with the dragon, but you didn't," Greg explained, his voice deceptively calm. "Because of that and our history together, I won't kill you."

Greg walked forward, lifting his mask once again. "I'm not happy about what you tried to do here, Joey, but I don't hate you for it. Call it misguided heroism. Call it a momentary lapse of common sense. Whatever you want to call it, I hope it's done now."

Turning away, the Puppet Master walked toward the edge of the roof again. He peered down on the gathered throngs of police and civilians, watching what had to have been a mystical combat between two Supers.

"I made the offer earlier for you to leave with your girlfriend. It still stands but not for too much longer. Please, listen to me this time and just leave. Go back to living your life in obscurity."

Joey thought about Danica, surely frightened for him a few floors beneath their feet. He thought of the civilians and police watching hundreds of feet below, hoping and praying that the Supers would simply kill one another for all their sake. His thoughts drifted to the lack of personal responsibility that permeated everything in Belltown.

He raised his head and stared at the Puppet Master.

"What will you do?" he asked.

Greg turned from the edge of the roof and smiled softly. "Does it matter? I mean to you. Does it matter to you?"

"All this will make you, what, Mayor of Belltown?" Joey asked, not answering Greg's questions.

The Puppet Master guffawed at the thought of being mayor.

"Then what?" Joey continued. "President? *King* Greg?"

Joey's hand drifted beneath the leather bracer on his wrist and felt the cards concealed within.

"Yeah, I'm going to take it all over. Maybe I will make myself king. King Greg has a pretty good ring to it, don't you think?"

Joey frowned sadly as he inched the cards closer to the surface. His eyes reflected the deep regret he felt in his heart.

"I was really hoping you wouldn't say that," he explained with a heavy sigh.

From beneath the bracer, he withdrew the first card and flung it toward his old friend. Greg deftly snatched the card from the air and held it up so he could see. Staring back at him was a plain 'Ace of Hearts'.

"I don't get it," Greg replied perplexed. "Is this your proverbial ace up your sleeve?"

Joey shook his head. "That one was a distraction. This one is my ace."

Holding up the Ace's pair, Joey showed the Puppet Master the 'King of Hearts' in his hand.

"I don't get it?" Greg said angrily.

"You wouldn't, *King* Greg. The 'King of Hearts' is better known as the '*Suicide* King'."

The surface of the card shimmered.

Wordlessly, Greg dropped the 'Ace of Hearts' onto the rooftop as he turned back toward the roof's edge. Walking forward, he didn't break stride as he stepped cleanly from the building's edge.

The building lurched violently as it tried to catch its master in mid fall, but it moved far too slowly. The Puppet Master plummeted the forty stories before striking the concrete sidewalk.

Immediately, the building settled back into its foundation as it lost its puppet status.

Emotional, Joey sat down on the roof and cried a silent prayer to his lost friend. For long minutes, he sat by himself as his mind tried to wrap itself around what he just did.

Finally, he pushed himself back to his feet and entered the building. By the time he found Danica and they made their way to the ground floor, they were able to fade into the hundreds of other hostages fleeing the Montrose building.

In the chaos, they were both able to slip away unnoticed by the police and fade back into obscurity.

ABOUT THE AUTHOR

Jon Messenger serves as a United States Army Officer in the Medical Service Corps. His passion for science fiction writing began during his college years at the University of Southern California and has grown through two combat deployments to Iraq and a humanitarian assistance mission in Haiti. He currently lives with his wife and son in Maryland.

Printed in Great Britain
by Amazon